For Dada, Harish Johari

Bear Cub Books
One Park Street
Rochester, Vermont 05767
www.InnerTraditions.com

Bear Cub Books is a division of Inner Traditions International

Text copyright © 2005 by Vatsala Sperling
Artwork copyright © 2005 by Pieter Weltevrede

LIBRARY OF CONGRESS CATALOGING-IN-PUBLICATION DATA

Sperling, Vatsala, 1961–
    Ram the demon slayer / Vatsala Sperling ; illustrated by Pieter Weltevrede.
        p. cm.
    Based on the Ramayana, adapted for children.
        Summary: Prince Ram, reincarnation of the heavenly god Vishnu, defeats the ten-headed demon king Ravana, who, with his army, has ransacked the earth.
    ISBN 1-59143-057-7
    1. Rama (Hindu deity)—Juvenile literature. 2. Hindu stories. [1. Rama (Hindu deity)
3. Folklore—India.] I. Weltevrede, Pieter, ill. II. Valmiki. Ramayana. III. Title.
    BL1139.25.S74 2005
    294.5'92204521—dc22

                                                                                2005023537

Printed and bound in China

10 9 8 7 6 5 4 3 2 1

Text design and layout by Virginia Scott Bowman
This book was typeset in Berkeley with Apple Chancery and Abbess as the display typefaces

Ram the Demon Slayer

Vatsala Sperling

Illustrated by Pieter Weltevrede

Bear Cub Books
Rochester, Vermont

At the southern tip of India, among the tall and mighty waves of the Indian Ocean, lay nestled the small island country of Lanka. This beautiful island was blessed with azure skies, green forests, and golden beaches. But Lanka's ruler was Ravana, a terrible demon with ten hideous heads and a mean and greedy spirit. Whenever he wanted, he could sprout twenty arms as well. He also happened to be the grandson of the mighty God of Creation, Lord Brahma.

Not content with his many powers, Ravana prayed to Brahma, insisting, "Make me immortal! Let no god or demon, animal or plant harm me!"

Brahma raised his eyebrows and asked, "What about humans?"

Ravana raised a dozen fists and sneered. "They have only two little arms, Grandfather. I have no fear of them."

So Brahma did as Ravana requested. And things on Earth went from bad to worse, as Ravana and his fellow demons went on one rampage after another. Desperate cries for help could be heard from all corners of the earth. Finally Brahma had had enough. He called on his fellow deity, Lord Vishnu, God of Preservation. Pointing down at Lanka, he said, "Since I granted Ravana eternal protection, there's nothing I can do to stop his cruelty. But, he was arrogant enough to think he would be safe from all men. If you go in human form, you will be able to destroy him once and for all."

Vishnu readily agreed. He had already been born on Earth many times to fight other demons, and quite enjoyed life as a human. Of course, his wife, Goddess Lakshmi, would be born on Earth, too. No matter where Lord Vishnu incarnated on Earth, Lakshmi always found him and they always got married to each other.

Soon enough, Vishnu picked out his new earthly family. The kingdom of Ayodhya was ruled by a wise and just king, Dasharatha, whose one deep regret had always been that he had no children. Following the advice of a holy sage, the king performed a sacred fire ceremony, praying to the gods with all his heart for children. And there, in the midst of the flames, a divine being appeared, offering Dasharatha a golden bowl filled with sweet rice pudding.

"Take this gift from the gods, and give it to your wives," the being said, "and your childless days will be over."

The three queens ate every bite, and before long all of them became mothers. Kausalya, the gentle and pious first queen, gave birth to Ram, the incarnation of Lord Vishnu. Kaikeyi, the valiant second queen, had once saved the king's life in battle. She named her baby Bharat. He was the incarnation of Lord Vishnu's conch shell and represented the clear voice of truth. The youngest queen, Sumitra, gave birth to twins, Lakshman and Shatrughn. Lakshman was the incarnation of Lord Vishnu's serpent, the fierce and faithful Shesha, while Shatrughn was the incarnation of Lord Vishnu's powerful mace.

With four babies to care for now, the new parents were happily occu-
pied. Soon the babies grew into lively, high-spirited little boys, and then
into handsome, intelligent young men. The royal counselor, Sage Vasistha,
was responsible for their education, and under his tutelage, they learned
how to govern like kings, ready to take any challenge. And this was a very
good thing, for soon enough their skills would be put to the test.

One afternoon there came a desperate pounding at the palace door. It was Sage Viswamitra. "We need help! Our forests are overrun with terrible demons!" he cried. "Send Ram with me. He can get rid of them."

Dasharatha was reluctant to let his sons go, but Ram accepted the challenge calmly, and he and Lakshman followed Sage Viswamitra into the dense and dangerous wood. As they walked, the path grew darker, and the air grew cold and silent. Ram listened for signs of life, but there were none. "O Sage, what has happened here?" he asked gravely.

"You are in the land of the demon Tataka. She has stripped the forest of all living things. The rivers and streams have dried up. Now she eats anyone who passes by." Then the sage drew a quick, harsh breath. "Watch out," he hissed in warning. "Here she comes."

They turned to see a huge, misshapen demon, her crooked fingers reaching toward them, her dreadful snout hungrily sniffing the air. Quickly, Ram let fly an arrow straight at her heart. With a long howl, she fell across the path. A sigh of relief rose from the floor of the parched forest as the demon died. In the distance, a bird began to sing.

"Well done," said the sage, breathing his own sigh of relief. "But beware," he continued. "There are other demons who use trickery and deceit. You will need sacred weapons."

They found a quiet spot at the bank of a river. As the sage began reciting secret mantras, the sacred weapons appeared. Ram sat motionless. Gleaming swords and burnished shields, glistening arrows and spears, one by one, merged into his body. He was aglow with divine power.

Suddenly, the sky turned ominously dark. The air filled with the sound of roaring thunder. This was no storm, however. It was two demons, Maricha and Subahu. This monstrous pair was in the habit of bothering humans with all sorts of mischief. One of their favorite tricks was to grind up the remains of dead animals and pour the horrid stuff all over people when they gathered to pray to the gods.

"I'll take care of them," said Lakshman grimly, fitting a deadly arrow to his bow. But Ram put out his hand to stop him.

"No, Lakshman," he said. "These demons are only causing mischief. The punishment must fit the crime." Ram let loose his own magic arrow, which snagged the two meddlesome creatures and carried them up through the air, over the mountaintops, right to the middle of the ocean. There it let them go, and—*splash*—they fell into the water, spluttering in surprise, but unhurt.

"Well done," said the sage again.

On their way back to Ayodhya, Sage Viswamitra said they would stop at the palace of King Janak, ruler of Mithila. The sage told them Janak's story as they walked along the winding trail through the forest. King Janak, like Dasharatha, had longed for a child for many years. One day, around the same time that Ram and his brothers were born, the king found a golden pitcher buried in his garden. Lying inside was a beautiful baby girl. With heartfelt thanks to Mother Earth, he named the baby Sita, and raised her as his own. Several years later, Lord Shiva paid Janak a visit and gave the king his own bow and arrow. He told Janak to keep it safe until Sita was old enough to marry. "Let each suitor try his hand. Only Lord Vishnu can lift up this bow and break it in two. Vishnu, and no other, will marry your daughter."

When Sage Viswamitra and the princes entered King Janak's court, they found him slumped over in despair. "Will my daughter ever find a husband?" the king groaned, as a host of suitors staggered about, complaining and moaning about their unsuccessful attempts to lift the bow. Viswamitra asked Ram to try.

Ram approached and bowed humbly, first to the king, then to the sage, and finally to the sacred weapon. Then, with one easy and fluid motion, he picked up the bow, fitted an arrow, and pulled the string. The arrow sped to the sky, and with a resounding *crack* the bow snapped into two pieces. The other suitors gaped in surprise. King Janak was delighted and relieved. His daughter, Sita, blushed quietly with happiness as Ram smiled in her direction.

"Very well done," said the sage, clapping his hands.

Amidst pomp and gaiety, Sita and Ram were married. They made a splendid couple. After all, theirs was a match made in heaven.

13

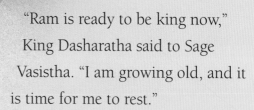

"Ram is ready to be king now,"
King Dasharatha said to Sage
Vasistha. "I am growing old, and it
is time for me to rest."

The news of Ram's forthcoming
coronation spread quickly through the
kingdom of Ayodhya. All the citizens
danced in the street. All but one, that is. Queen
Kaikeyi's maid, Manthara, was a malicious and
unpleasant old woman who collected grudges like other
people collect trinkets. She never forgave anyone for anything.
When Ram was just a little boy, he had flung a mud pie at her by mistake.
How the memory still stung! She had vowed to put him in his place one
day. And his place, she decided, would definitely not be the throne!
So, that evening, as she brushed Queen Kaikeyi's hair, she said, "I hear
Ram has been chosen as the next king. You must be very disappointed,
for Bharat's sake."

"Why do you say that? Ram will be a great king," said Kaikeyi.
"Besides, Bharat is second son."

The two women's eyes met in the mirror. Kaikeyi sighed and said,
"The son of the first queen inherits the throne. Nothing can change
the law."

"My most honorable queen," Manthara said slyly, "do you not
remember how you saved the king's life on the battlefield so long ago?
Do you not remember his promise to you?"

"What are you trying to say?" asked the queen.

"He will grant you anything. Two wishes . . ." whispered Manthara. "Do this for Bharat! Ask the king to banish Ram from the land for fourteen years and give the throne to Bharat." Manthara's eyes glittered with malice.

"Leave me alone, Manthara!" Kaikeyi cried in confusion. The old maid set down the brush and crept from the room. Then she rubbed her gnarled hands together with evil glee.

When King Dasharatha knocked at Queen Kaikeyi's door he found her distraught, sprawled on the floor with her long black hair in tangles. "What's the matter, my brave young queen?" the king asked gently. "What can I do to help?"

"You once promised you would give me anything," the queen said in a low voice.

"Of course I remember, dearest. I owe you my life," the king said soothingly.

"Then banish Ram from the land for fourteen years," Kaikeyi said, "and make Bharat the next king." There was a long ominous silence.

Finally the king spoke. "You cannot be asking this."

"Yes, I can," said the queen.

The king's voice cracked with sorrow. "Then I must keep my promise."

In the morning, the king sent for Ram. But his grief was too great, and he was unable to speak. Finally Kaikeyi explained the king's promise. Ram took in the situation calmly, but Lakshman was furious with this news.

"Lakshman, do not speak ill of our mother Kaikeyi. And dearest Father," he said gently, turning to the king. "I am relieved it is nothing more serious. I will gladly honor your promise to Kaikeyi. Please, do not worry."

But the poor king was inconsolable. "Son," he cried, "fourteen years is too long a time. I am an old man. I am afraid I will never see you again."

It was a terrible time for the kingdom. Ram left on his long journey, accompanied by Sita and Lakshman. And soon after, the good King Dasharatha died of a broken heart. Bharat, who had been visiting his grandfather, returned to a cloud of gloom. When he learned what had happened, he confronted his mother, his clear voice ringing with the truth. "You were wrong to ask this of our father. I do not want to be king. I will find Ram in the forest and ask him to return to his rightful place on the throne."

But when Bharat found Ram in the wilderness, Ram would not agree to return. He had promised to honor his father's word and no amount of cajoling could persuade him to change his mind. So in the end Bharat brought Ram's sandals home and placed them on the royal throne. For the next fourteen years he ruled Ayodhya as Ram's representative.

Meanwhile, Ram, Lakshman, and Sita sought haven in the dense Panchavati forest near the Godavari River. They chose a small clearing in the woods and Lakshman built a cottage. "We will be safe here," he said, looking around with satisfaction.

But no one is ever safe from the demons. The first to find them was
the demon Shurpanakha, Ravana's younger sister. She arrived in the form
of a slender young maiden, smiling flirtatiously, and looking from one to
another. "Marry me, handsome prince," she said to Ram, "I am all
yours." But Ram and Lakshman saw through her guise at once.
Lakshman shot her with an arrow, chopping off her nose.
She changed quickly into her true demon form. "You
will pay for this, Lakshman!" Shurpanakha cried.

Next came the army of Khara and Dushana,
Shurpanakha's older brothers. But Ram was
ready, showering the advancing demons with
divine deadly fire. Shurpanakha witnessed
this disaster and rushed off to see Ravana.
She told him everything that had
happened. "You must avenge the
insult to me! Avenge the death of our
brothers! Kill the mortals! Take the
beautiful maiden as your prize!" she
yelled angrily.

At the mention of the beautiful
maiden, Ravana sat up. "The
men will die," he declared,
waving several arms
in the air. A greedy
smile spread over
each of his
faces. "And
the girl will
be mine!"

Ravana summoned his uncle Maricha—the same Maricha who had been dumped in the ocean by Ram's magic arrow. Although Maricha warned his nephew of Ram's divine powers, Ravana ordered Maricha to help capture Sita. Together they devised a foolproof plan. Maricha turned himself into a dazzlingly lovely deer, dancing lightly through the forest, luring Ram from the cottage. Once out of sight, the deer mimicked Ram's voice, crying "Lakshman, help me! O Sita, help!"

Sita insisted that Lakshman go at once to help Ram. But before he went, Lakshman drew a line across the threshold and told Sita to stay inside where she'd be safe. With the parting words, "Remember, don't cross this line," he left to go to Ram's aid.

As soon as Lakshman was out of sight, Ravana appeared at the door in the guise of a hermit asking for food. When he tried to step across Lakshman's line he found that flames licked up and burned his toes, so he called sweetly, "Please come out with the food, O Lady. It wouldn't be proper for me to enter the house."

As Sita stepped out with a basket of fruit, Ravana returned to demon form and grabbed her roughly by the arm, pulling her into a magic chariot. "I am Ravana, the demon king!" he cried. "Now you must come with me to Lanka!"

Sita looked in horror at Ravana's ten leering heads and screamed, "Let me go, let me go!" But the chariot took off into the air with poor Sita hanging over the side, crying desperately for help.

Jatayu, King of the Vultures, soaring above on the warm winds, heard Sita's pitiful cries. He swooped down to rescue her, but Ravana pulled his sword and chopped off the brave bird's wings. This brought fresh tears to Sita's eyes. But then she spied a few monkeys sitting on a hilltop. She took her jewelry off, tied it into a bundle, and threw it down. The monkeys looked up to see the chariot and heard her calling Ram's name.

Meanwhile, back at the cottage, Ram and Lakshman had returned to find Sita gone. There were signs of a struggle. Squashed and broken fruits were scattered over the ground. Ram turned to Lakshman, his face drained of color. "What has become of my beloved Sita?" he cried.

The brothers set off immediately, and soon came upon Jatayu, lying mortally wounded in the bushes. "Ravana has taken Sita to Lanka. Hurry! I tried my best, but . . . I'm so sorry," gasped Jatayu, and breathed his last.

Ram and Lakshman gave the valiant vulture king a decent burial, then hastened farther south. They were encouraged when they met the monkey Hanuman, son of the wind god, who took them to meet the king of the monkeys, Sugriva. They found Sita's bag of jewels there, with the monkey king.

Sugriva lived in exile after losing his kingdom and his wife to his wicked older brother. So Ram and Sugriva promised to help each other. Ram would go after Sugriva's brother and Sugriva would send search parties in every direction to look for Sita.

"You go to Lanka," Ram said to Hanuman. He gave Hanuman his royal ring, saying, "Take this. You might need it."

Hanuman had a special boon that enabled him to fly through the sky at the speed of lightning, and to change his size and form as he pleased. He jumped over the ocean, reaching the beautiful island of Lanka in the blink of an eye. But as he swung through the trees of the forest, he came upon something very unsightly indeed. A ten-headed demon crashed through the underbrush, an entourage of grisly monsters behind him. This ugly creature stopped under the very tree where Hanuman was perched, and began to speak in a loud, unpleasant voice. Hanuman peered through the leaves and saw a beautiful young woman sitting at the base of the trunk.

"Marry me! Marry me!" the demon shouted. The woman answered angrily. "You come here day after day and make the same ridiculous demand. I will never marry you. One day my husband, Ram, will kill you on the battlefield."

Grumbling, the demon slouched away. Hanuman jumped down from the tree. "Salutations, Sita. I am Ram's servant, Hanuman." He showed her Ram's signet ring.

Sita's face cleared. She smiled, but said urgently, "Tell my husband to hurry! Only he can set me free!"

Hanuman sped back to Ram with the good news. King Sugriva and all his monkeys hooted with joy. With the help of Jambavan, king of the bears, they organized an army of monkeys and bears and began the march south. When they reached the ocean, Ram offered a prayer to the ocean god.

"My monkeys cannot swim," he said. "Please, show us the way to Lanka." In reply, the ocean god told them to gather rocks lying on the beach, and carve Ram's name on them.

"Now throw them into my waters," the ocean god instructed. The rocks bobbed like buoys on the sea and the army of monkeys and bears stepped across lightly all the way to Lanka.

Ravana's spies brought him news of the invaders. "Ram has four battalions—one at each of our gates!" they reported.

Ravana dismissed the news with a shake of his ten ugly heads. "Those puny men and their pet monkeys cannot harm me! I am immortal!" roared the demon king.

"Your brother, Prince Vibhishana, has surrendered to Ram and joined his camp," they reported.

Ravana dismissed the news with a wave of his twenty hands. "I don't need his help. He was always sitting around praying to Vishnu. What a goody-goody! We will attack today!"

Ravana's army came on horses and elephants. The monkeys
and bears fought bravely and well, but they were no match for
demon magic and deception. As night came on, the demons became more
sneaky; after all, they were the creatures of darkness. They would appear to
fall down dead, only to pop up in another place. They mocked the monkeys
and chopped them up like vegetables. But still, the battle raged on.

"We must conquer them once and for all!" shouted Ravana.

The demons tried one ruse after another. First Ravana's son Indrajeet sent a magic arrow that covered Ram and Lakshman with a blanket of poisonous snakes. But Garuda, Lord Vishnu's pet eagle, untangled the coiled mass and pulled them off of the warriors. Next, Ravana awoke his other brother, the enormous demon Kumbhakarna. Kumbhakarna had a ravenous appetite. He often slept for six months at a time, but when he woke up, *watch out*—he'd be so hungry he could eat all of Ram's army for a snack—and Ravana was hoping that he would. But like their brother Vibhishana, Kumbhakarna was pious. He was devoted to Lord Shiva. He could see that Ravana was in the wrong and he didn't want to fight Ram. Nevertheless, Ravana ordered him to go, and so, tossing a few cartloads of raw meat down his throat, he clomped into battle. Ram heard the giant's heavy footsteps in the distance, and fitted his bow with Lord Shiva's special arrow. Kumbhakarna died instantly. An entire regiment of monkeys scattered as his body crashed to the ground.

Ravana raged and stormed about the palace when he heard the news. "Can no one rid me of Ram?" he cried.

"Father, I will use my Brahmastra," said Indrajeet. "Great-grandfather Brahma gave it to me. My magic arrows can decimate an entire army in no time," Indrajeet boasted as he headed for the battleground.

And Brahmastra, the most powerful of all god-given weapons, did just what Indrajeet claimed. With a shower of arrows, Brahmastra put a spell on the entire army. Ram, Lakshman, and all their soldiers fell into a deep trance, hovering at the edge of death.

Only one of the entire army remained awake. The bear king, Jambavan, was a son of Lord Brahma, so he was not affected. Also, Jambavan was a healer who knew everything about the medicinal powers of herbs. He roused Hanuman from the spell, and carefully described the herbs he needed to restore life and heal wounds. "Go! Quickly, Hanuman," he said. "The herbs grow only on Sanjeevani Mountain in the foothills of the Himalayas."

Hanuman leaped over the Indian Ocean to the foothills of the Himalayas in a single swift bound. He found Sanjeevani Mountain covered with a dense forest of herbs. But it was quite dark by then, and the plants all looked the same to Hanuman. "Triangular leaves, purple flowers," he muttered to himself. "I can't tell them apart!" Finally, he began to dig at the base of the mountain. He dug until the mountain itself was loosened from the earth around it and he found that he could pick up the whole mountain and hold it in the palm of his hand.

"Aha! The entire mountain and all of its herbs wish to be of service to Ram," he said, and taking a deep breath, he rose up into the sky. With the mountain resting on his palm, he zoomed back to Lanka.

The fragrance
of the medicinal
herbs reached the island
shores even before Hanuman
did, stirring many soldiers back
to life. Jambavan urged them to pick up the dead demons and
throw them into the ocean. Ram, whom Brahma
himself had already released from the spell, praised
the strength and faithfulness of his animal friends
and soldiers.

Jambavan then prepared amazing concoctions
from the chosen herbs and went from one soldier
to the next, offering a dose here, a poultice
there, or a few leaves to chew. Rows
of wounded and dying soldiers
awoke as if from sleep,
without so much as
a scratch left on
their bodies.

The next morning Indrajeet was back on the battlefield. He had expected to spend the day victoriously counting up the dead, but instead, Lakshman stood before him.

"Run," said Lakshman. "Run for your life."

But Indrajeet mocked him. "You can't fool me. You're just a ghost. Don't you even know you're already dead?"

In reply, Lakshman pulled out his bow. The arrow neatly sliced off Indrajeet's head and carried it all the way to Ravana. "Father, set Sita free," the severed head moaned. "Your enemies are no mere mortals. Give up, father."

"Only after I avenge your death, my dearest son," Ravana roared—and he rushed into battle, himself.

It was a long and bloody fight. One after another, Ram called upon the sacred weapons and aimed them at Ravana. One after another, he cut off the demon's many heads and arms. But as soon as he cut off one head, another would spring up in its place. In the blink of an eye, the demon's severed arms and legs grew back.

Ravana seemed to have an infinite capacity to heal and regenerate himself. Ram fought all day without making any progress at all. In ancient India, battles were fought only from sunrise to sunset. Ram tossed and turned all night, wondering how he could destroy this seemingly immortal being.

Help came just as the first rays of the dawn touched the sands, when the wise sage Agastya appeared before Ram. "Even the gods need divine assistance when they take human form," Agastya said. Under the early morning sky Sage Agastya taught Ram special prayers for the Sun god. "Chant these mantras. Don't give up; evil is not immortal," he said. After performing his salutations to the sun, Ram headed back to the battlefield with renewed confidence. All through the day he used his heavenly weapons and called to Ravana to surrender.

But Ravana refused. "I am immortal!" he shouted, and continued to sprout new heads and limbs like so many weeds. Finally, in the long light of the afternoon, Ram knew that it was time to finish the battle. He aimed one last arrow straight into Ravana's belly button, piercing the very center of the demon's spirit.

With a look of shock and astonishment, Ravana fell. And this time, he did not get up again. The mightiest of all demons was dead, slain finally by a man who was also a god—Lord Vishnu—in human form.

Cries of "Victory to Ram the Demon Slayer," rose from every corner of the battlefield. The monkeys leaped into the air and danced. The surviving demons gladly surrendered, promising to give up their wicked ways forever.

Ram's fourteen-year exile was over at last. Good Prince Vibhishana took over the rule of Lanka from his slain demon brother Ravana, and Ram, Sita, and Lakshman returned to Ayodhya, where Ram took his rightful place on the throne. His long and prosperous rule is still remembered in India as the "golden age of Indian civilization."

Note to Parents and Teachers

The Ramayana is one of the oldest and greatest Indian epics. Though it was written thousands of years ago, its hero, Ram, is loved and respected in India to this day. What is it about Ram that has appealed to so many generations? First and foremost, it is his humility. Despite his godly origins, when he is born on Earth as a human prince Ram obeys the laws of nature and society just like anyone else. Aware of his human limitations, he courts, and gracefully accepts, help from all beings: gods and sages, plants and animals, rocks, and the water of the ocean itself.

In India, Ram is seen as the embodiment of truth and virtue—the highest of human values. He represents respect for parents and teachers, love for siblings and friends, and compassion for the weak and downtrodden. He honors spoken words and promises, which makes him trustworthy and reliable, and his bravery in the face of danger makes him stand tall among people of all ages, and throughout the centuries, as the ideal hero.

About the Illustrations

The original illustrations were created with watercolor and tempera paints. Using transparent watercolors the artist painted each picture in several steps. After outlining the figures, he filled them in, using three tones for each color to achieve a three-dimensional effect; next he applied the background colors. After each step he "fixed" the painting by pouring water over it until only the paint absorbed by the paper remained.

Then the artist applied a "wash," using opaque tempera paints. After wetting the painting again, he applied the tempera to the surface until the whole painting appeared to be behind a colored fog. While the wash color was still wet, he used a dry brush to remove it from the faces, hands, and feet of the figures. He let the wash dry completely, then rinsed it again to fix the colors. The paintings received several washes and fixes before the right color and emotional tone was achieved. Finally, he redefined the delicate line work of each piece, allowing the painting to reemerge from within the clouds of wash.

Please feel free to trace or photocopy this line drawing of Ram for children to color.